The
Wind
in the
Willows

The
Wind
in the
Willows

Kenneth Grahame

Illustrated by E.H. Shepard

Abridged by David McDowall

JS

This edition first published in Great Britain 1999
by Methuen Children's Books
an imprint of Egmont Children's Books Limited
239 Kensington High Street, London, W8 6SA

The Wind in the Willows originally published
1908 by Methuen & Co Ltd.
Line illustrations copyright Ernest H. Shepard
under the Berne Convention.
Colouring of the illustrations copyright
© 1970, 1971, by Ernest H. Shepard and
Methuen Children's Books Ltd.
Text copyright © Kenneth Grahame 1908

0 7497 3937 1

10 9 8 7 6 5 4 3 2

A CIP catalogue record for this book is available
from the British Library

Printed in Spain by Gráficas Estella

CONTENTS

THE RIVER BANK

$\mathcal{M}$ole had been spring cleaning. His arms were tired, spring was in the air, and he flung his brush down and cried, "Hang spring cleaning!"

He bolted out of his house, scraped with his paws, muttering, "Up we go! Up we go!" till at last pop! his snout came into the sunlight and he was rolling in the warm grass. Off he jumped in the joy of spring without its cleaning.

Mole found himself at the edge of a river. Never had he seen one before. There was a hole in the bank opposite, in which a face with whiskers suddenly appeared. It was Water Rat.

"Hullo, Mole!" said Rat. "Would you like to come over?"

Mole soon found himself sitting in a boat.

"Do you know," Mole said, "I've never been in a boat before."

"What? Never been in a – well, I never – there is nothing half so much worth doing as messing about in boats. Supposing we make a long day of it?"

Rat climbed into his hole and reappeared with a fat wicker basket.

"What's inside it?" asked Mole, wriggling with curiosity.

"There's cold chicken," replied Rat briefly, "coldtonguecold hamcoldbeefpickledgherkinssaladfrenchrollscresssandwidges pottedmeatgingerbeerlemonadesodawater–"

"O stop, stop," cried Mole. "This is too much!"

Leaving the main stream, they entered a beautiful backwater. Mole could only gasp, "O my! O my! O my!"

Rat helped Mole ashore, and they were soon tucking into their picnic.

The afternoon sun was getting low as Rat rowed homewards.

"Ratty! Please, I want to row now!" Mole cried.

Ratty shook his head. "Not yet – it's not so easy as it looks."

Mole was quiet for a minute or two, feeling jealous of Rat. Suddenly he jumped up and seized the oars and made a dig at the water. He missed, his legs flew out over his head and – Sploosh! he found himself in the river. How cold the water was, and how wet.

Then a paw gripped the back of his neck. It was Rat.

Mole, wet without and ashamed within, trotted about till he was dry. "Ratty," he said in a low voice, "I am very sorry indeed for my foolish conduct."

"That's all right, bless you!" responded Ratty cheerfully. "I'll teach you to row and to swim, and you'll soon be as handy on the water as any of us."

Mole was so touched that he had to brush away a tear or two with the back of his paw. Rat kindly looked the other way.

When they got home, Rat made a bright fire and planted Mole in an armchair in front of it. Before long he escorted a sleepy but contented Mole upstairs to bed.

The horse reared and plunged and, in spite of Mole's efforts, drove the cart backwards into a ditch. It wavered an instant – then there was a crash – and the cart, their pride and joy, lay on its side, a wreck.

Rat danced up and down in the road. "Villains," he shouted, shaking both fists, "you scoundrels, you . . . you . . . roadhogs!"

Rat and Mole quietened the horse, but couldn't right the cart. Toad sat in a trance, his eyes fixed on the dusty wake of their destroyer.

"Glorious sight!" he murmured. "The *real* way to travel! The *only* way to travel! And to think I never knew!"

"What are we going to do with him?" asked Mole.

"Nothing at all," replied Rat firmly, "because there is really nothing to be done now he has got a new craze. Now, Toad!" said Rat sharply. "Once we get to town, you'll have to go straight to the police station and complain, and then arrange for the cart to be mended."

"Police station!" murmured Toad dreamily. "Complain about that heavenly vision! Mend the cart! I've done with carts forever!"

Rat turned to Mole. "You see, he's quite hopeless."

The following evening Rat met Mole on the river bank.

"Heard the news?" Rat said. "Toad took the train to Town this morning and has ordered a large and very expensive motor car."

BADGER &
THE WILD WOOD

*M*ole wanted to meet Badger, but Rat always put him off, saying, "He's shy, besides he lives in the middle of the Wild Wood. We river-bankers don't go there very much. There are Weasels and Stoats in the Wild Wood and you can't trust them and that's the fact."

It was now winter. One afternoon, as Rat dozed before the fire, Mole decided to go by himself to explore the Wild Wood and perhaps find Badger.

It was cold with a steely sky overhead. The country lay bare and leafless. Mole cheerfully made for the Wild Wood which lay ahead, low and threatening.

There was nothing to alarm him at first. He penetrated where the light was less, and trees crouched nearer and nearer. Everything was very still.

Then the faces began.

He thought he saw an evil face looking out at him from a hole. He told himself not to begin imagining things. He strode on but suddenly every hole seemed to possess a face.

Then the whistling began.

Very faint and shrill, but it made him hurry forward. They were up and alert, whoever they were. And he – he was alone and unarmed, far from help and with the night closing in.

Then the pattering began. He thought it was only falling leaves at first. Then it grew into a regular rhythm. A rabbit bolted past him, crying, "Get out, you fool!" as he disappeared down a burrow.

Mole began running he knew not whither. At last he took refuge in the hollow of an old beech tree, panting and trembling with the Terror of the Wild Wood!

Meanwhile, Rat had awoken to find Mole gone. Outside he saw footprints running purposefully to the Wild Wood. Rat looked grave. He re-entered the house, strapped a belt around his waist, stuck a brace of pistols into it and took up a cudgel and set off for the Wild Wood at a smart pace.

It was dusk when he reached the wood. He hunted patiently calling out, "Moly, Moly, Moly! It's me – Rat!"

At last he heard a little cry, "Ratty, is that really you?" Mole was cheered by the sound of Rat's voice and the sight of his stick and pistols.

"Now," said Rat, "we must make a start for home."

But by now it was snowing hard and everything looked different. They set off but an hour or two later they pulled up, weary and hopelessly lost. The snow was so deep they could hardly drag their little legs through it.

Suddenly Mole tripped and fell with a squeal.

"O, my poor shin!" he cried.

"Let's see, Mole," said Rat. "It's a clean cut. Looks as if it was made by a sharp metal edge. Funny!" He scratched around and suddenly cried "Hooray!" and danced a jig in the snow.

"What have you found, Ratty? A doorscraper! Why dance around a doorscraper that some careless person has left lying around?"

"Stop talking and scrape!" cried Rat, digging with fury. Rat's cudgel struck something hollow, a little green door with an iron bell-pull beside it and a brass plate which read:

MR BADGER

Mole fell back in surprise and delight.

"Rat! You're a wonder. You worked it out the moment I cut my shin!"

"Get up and ring that doorbell there as hard as you can!" cried Rat.

Mole clutched it and swung there. A long way off they could hear the deep-toned bell respond.

Finally they heard a bolt shoot back and a long snout appeared and a pair of sleepy blinking eyes.

"O Badger," cried Rat, "let us in, please. It's me, Rat, and my friend Mole, and we've lost our way in the snow."

"Come in both of you at once," cried Badger. "Why, you must be perished."

The two animals tumbled inside. Badger settled them by the fire, and then summoned them to the table where he had prepared a sumptuous meal. After supper, Badger asked for news of Toad.

"O, he's going from bad to worse," said Rat gravely. "Another smash-up only last week, his seventh. We're his friends – oughtn't we to do something?"

"Well," said Badger, "in the spring we'll take Toad seriously in hand. We'll bring him back to reason. We'll make him be a sensible Toad."

But Rat was already half asleep.

After lunch the next day Rat said, "Come along, Mole, we must be off. Don't want to spend another night in the Wild Wood."

Badger took them along an underground short cut. At last daylight showed through the passage. Badger bade them goodbye and they found themselves standing on the very edge of the Wild Wood, ahead of them in the distance the welcome glint of the river.